Sleepy, the Goodnight Buddy

By
Drew Daywalt

Illustrated by
Scott Campbell

Disney • Hyperion
Los Angeles   New York

Roderick hated going to bed.

Each night he would think of every possible excuse to try to stay up longer.

Sometimes he would ask for another story.
Sometimes he would ask for a drink of water.

Sometimes he would ask for a pony. He never got a pony—but that's okay, because he didn't really want one. He just wanted to stay up, even if it was just to hear all the reasons why he couldn't have a pony.
And there were lots of reasons.

We don't have a barn.

Ponies won't use a litter box.

Ponies hog the bed.

Ponies watch the TV too loud.

But he would always ask for something, anything, just to stay up a little bit longer.

Roderick's parents decided to get him a goodnight buddy to help him sleep.

He couldn't decide whether it looked more
like a moose or more like a bear.

"His name is Sleepy," said his mother.

"He's your goodnight buddy," said his father.
"He's going to help you fall asleep."

That night, Roderick's parents put Sleepy in bed with him.

But Sleepy kept staring at him.

Roderick decided to hide Sleepy.

He tried stashing him on the bookshelf . . .

behind the curtains . . .

and even under his pillow. . . .

But no matter where Roderick put him,
he could *FEEL* Sleepy looking at him.
Finally, Roderick picked him up and
tossed him into the closet.

"Wait!" said a quiet little voice from the darkness. "Don't leave me alone in here."

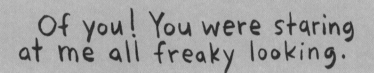

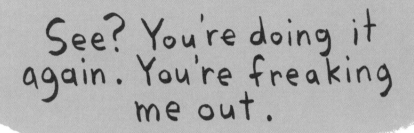

One day in class, Duncan went to take out his crayons and found a stack of letters with his name on them . . .

I'm not mad.
You sound mad. That sounds like you're mad.
I'm not mad... just tired.
Okay, I'm a little mad, but mostly I'm tired.
Well, I can't sleep even if you're a little mad.

SLEEPY!!! It's time for bed! Now go to sleep!
I'm sorry, Roderick. I guess I'm just not a very good "goodnight buddy."
Are you kidding? You're the worst goodnight buddy ever! You're supposed to take my mind off scary things and help me sleep, but instead you're just exhausting me!

Hey, Roderick?

To Abigail and Reese, *but mostly Reese*
—D.D.

For Sonny, August, and Audrey
—S.C.

First Edition, September 2018
1 3 5 7 9 10 8 6 4 2
FAC-029191-18166
Printed in Malaysia

Designed by Tyler Nevins
This book is set in Caecilia LT Pro/Monotype with hand-lettering by Scott Campbell.
The illustrations were created in watercolor with digital enhancement.

Library of Congress Cataloging-in-Publication Data

Names: Daywalt, Drew, author. • Campbell, Scott, 1973- illustrator.
Title: Sleepy, the goodnight buddy / by Drew Daywalt ; illustrated by Scott Campbell.
Description: First edition. • Los Angeles ; New York : Disney-Hyperion, 2018.
  • Summary: "When a boy who routinely refuses to go to bed gets a talkative stuffed animal, the tables are turned!"—Provided by publisher.
Identifiers: LCCN 2017048848 • ISBN 9781484789698
Subjects: • CYAC: Bedtime—Fiction. • Toys—Fiction.
Classification: LCC PZ7.D3388 Sl 2018 • DDC [E]—dc23
LC record available at https://lccn.loc.gov/2017048848

Reinforced binding
Visit www.DisneyBooks.com